Diary of A Desperate Mind

by

M. Queeni Green

Published in the United States by:
M. Queeni Green and
Queeni Sings Ministries
Post Office Box 2
Browns Mills, NJ 08015
www.queenisings.com

ISBN-13: 978-1626769397 (Print)
ISBN – 978-1-62676-929-8 (eBook)

DEDICATION

This book to dedicated to the RELEASE of all who are feeling desperate. I pray your HOPE for something better, leads you to connect to your FAITH, and it releases you to the LOVE what God has for you.

ACKNOWLEDGMENTS

First acknowledging and thanking my Lord and Savior Jesus Christ, the keeper and leader of my entire being. To my husband and children, for allowing me the creative space to do all the things the Lord is calling me to do. Thank you Crystal Lowe, for editing my first book. Rev. Dr. Angelita Clifton, for the insightful Foreword. Queeni Sings Ministries Team, for rising to every challenge and exceeding my expectations. Finally, to my ROLCWC church family, for always praying for your Pastor. #TheRiverFlows

Always, REACH for your dreams, EMBRACE every accomplishment, and ENJOY every blessing! I love you _**ALL**_ to life for life!

Foreword

22. Do not deceive yourselves by just listening to his word; instead, put it into practice. 23.If you listen to the word, but do not put it into practice you are like people who look in a mirror and see themselves as they are. 24. They take a good look at themselves and then go away and at once forget what they look like. 25. But if you look closely into the perfect law that sets people free, and keep on paying attention to it and do not simply listen and then forget it, but put it into practice— you will be blessed by God in what you do. **James 1:22-25** *The Good News Translation*

Upon meeting Reverend M. Queeni Green, the Pastor of the River of Life Worship Center, I was inspired by her commitment to God's call. Upon hearing her journey in ministry, I admired her passionate pursuit of God's plan. I believe there's no one better, than Pastor Queeni Green, to sermonize the push and pull of **Faith, Hope and Love.** "Diary of a Desperate Mind" is a lighthearted look into life's mirror, revealing the "heart-work" required to listen and live the Word. Whether you're desiring a mate, just wishing for material things or working in ministry, the Word goes to war with the world, when **Faith, Hope and Love** - three simple but profound virtues are wounded on the battlefields of life.

Let's be honest, anyone who's been a Christian for any length of time understands how **Faith, Hope and Love** can be like white noise, spiritual clichés— reduced to the level of meaningless "Christianese." The adversary is crafty, working from within, making both word and deed seem empty. Betrayed by our own emotions, watching the enemy turn **Faith, Hope and Love** into stones, imprisoning the head and the heart can be difficult. When a "not my will but thy will" mindset is consumed by "I want, what I want, when I want it" thinking, the urgency of now makes our vision more secular than sacred. When a carnal lens distorts our vision of the eternal, people and problems trump God's plan.

It's a fact, behavior flows naturally and almost effortlessly out of our core motivations. We can't help but live in light of what motivates us. When our beliefs are in constant conflict with our behavior, it's a telltale sign, our wants are no longer in line with God's will. Real spiritual transformation requires a renewed mind that realigns our attitudes and actions with God's will in light of His Word. Authentic spiritual maturity can be measured with one simple question: **How am I growing in Faith, in Hope and in Love?** When these important spiritual markers are absent or weak, we end up living selfish, self-centered, self serving lives that lead to spiritual destruction. Growing in **Faith, Hope and Love** allows Spirit-led beliefs to shape Spirit-led behavior, while living in God's pleasing and perfect plan. Remember, everyone who grows old, doesn't grow up. There's a big difference between age and maturity. Ideally, the older we are, the more spiritually mature we should be; but too often the ideal does not become the real. The result is one problem after another in our personal relationships, in our families and with our friends.

The epistle of James was written to help us understand and attain spiritual maturity: "... that ye may be perfect and entire, wanting nothing." James was addressing the suffering saints when he wrote, "Be patient." This was his counsel at the beginning of his letter (James 1: 1– 5) and his counsel as his letter came to a close. "Diary of a Desperate Mind" gives us a glimpse of manmade mishaps that turn into modern day miracles. This manuscript teaches life lessons learned as Mikayla realizes "I don't need a man; I want a man." Pastor Queeni Green makes it plain, a spiritually mature mind appreciates **Faith, Hope and Love** as virtues working in tandem, understanding that the greatest of these is **Love.**

Haven't we all, at one point or another, realized what we want isn't in line with God's will? Haven't we all been like Mikayla, out of alignment and out of order? Haven't we all seen an opportunity to live in God's will as the obstacle to living our lives? Pastor Queeni Green uses the storyline in "Diary of a Desperate Mind" to remind the reader that God's promises come, living His plan pursuing His purpose. If we understand every experience is preparing us for what He's prepared, we're blessed instead of burdened. Mikayla's story reminds us that life is like a box of chocolates, you never know what you're going to get, simply because God's ways are not our ways and His time is not our time. Like Mikayla our lives can change overnight when we understand God uses all things for the greater good of those who love Him and are called according to His word. I hear the Psalmist say trust in the Lord, commit yourself to Him and He will bring it to pass. God will never give a desire that takes us outside of His will, His work or His way. God is an ever-present help in a time of trouble. He's a wonderful counselor, who's always covering, comforting and caring for us—I hear Reverend Queeni Green proclaim... "Won't He Do it!!!" I must declare, Yes, Yes He Will!!!

Reverend Angelita Clifton, D. Min.
Associate Minister
Fountain Baptist Church
116 Glenside Avenue
Summit, New Jersey 07901

INTRODUCTION

This was written as a diary to share with you the day by day struggles we have as we journey toward happiness. There are many signs that a person is not right for us, yet we press to build a future with them anyway. We have many questions in our mind, and we never inquire with the person we are having reservations about. We find ourselves looking externally for answers from those closest to us.

STOP!!!!

Rely, only, on the LORD! Let His gentle hand lead, and guide you into the position, into the place, and to the person whom HE desires for you. When we do this, the struggle is not as hard, loving them becomes easy, and life is better because we are blessed in our obedience.

Open up right now in the name of Jesus, seek God for what you are to learn from this book, and enjoy the journey!!!!

CONTENTS

HELLO

Hello,

If you are reading this, one of two things has happened: 1. I have gone on to be with the Lord; or, 2. the unimaginable – I have lost an important piece of my legacy. If you have found this diary, READ IT... it is your destiny.

Allow me to take a moment to introduce myself. My name is Mikayla Yvonne Howard. I was born September 27, 1979 in Plainfield, NJ, to the late Michon Yvette Howard and James Leblanc. My mother died giving birth to me, and I was raised by my Grandparents, Michael and Queen Ester Howard. I attended the Plainfield Public School System, and graduated from Plainfield High School in 1997. I was very popular, a Cheerleader, and a member of Gospel Choir. After high school, I attended Florida State University in Tallahassee, FL., Graduating in the top 5% of my class in 2001, with a Bachelor's Degree in Music Therapy and Composition. I continued on, and received a Master's Degree in Music Teacher Education in 2004. I moved to Central Florida in 2004 and launched my business, "1 Stop Planning by Mikayla," and, I quickly became one of the most sought after Event Planners in the world; at least in my part of the world. I have had the pleasure of planning events for major corporations, and some of the most elite socialites from the east to west coasts. I am also one of the best background singers in the Gospel Music Industry, backing some of the greatest in the business including Donnie McClurkin, Yolanda Adams, Bishop Marvin Sapp, Tamela Mann, Kirk Franklin, and the list goes on. I have an entire chest of memorabilia for you to explore, enjoy, and journey through the fun I had traveling and doing what I love – singing and planning events.

My grandparents had two children, my mother – Michon and a son, Michael, Jr. Unfortunately, Michael and his wife, Keri, were killed in an accident in 1993. They had two children, Sandra and Darnell, fraternal twins. They came to live with us when they were thirteen years old. We all went to high school together and graduated the same year; however, we are not very close. I don't appreciate how they treated our Grandmother. I understand that our Grandmother did not like their mother very much, and they often bumped heads, but that same woman raised me to treat people

10

the way I want to be treated. My Grandmother stressed that we are to love everyone as the Lord has commanded us. I imagine their mother shared with them some of the troubles she experienced with Mama. But, it seems she neglected to teach them to love unconditionally, or to honor your mother and father that your days will be long upon the earth. Mama was sweet, but she didn't take any mess either. Just thinking about it reminds me of the time when my best friend, Myesha and I were making mud pies in the backyard and we took one inside for her and she said, "I love y'all dearly, but Mama don't eat mud pies!" She gave us a look that quickly sent us back outside.

I am 34 years old. I own my own home in Windermere, FL. I am a brilliant business owner, a 5-octave range backing vocalist, and I am a VIRGIN! That's right, I have never had sex. I had a high school sweetheart in high school, for now let's just call him "you know who," and we never consummated our relationship because we never married. In fact, I have never been married and promised the Lord and my Grandmother, that I would give myself only to my husband. I like to think of myself as funny, honest, and very committed. I have strong multi-tasking skills, and I love the Lord with every fiber of my being. I am book smart, and partially street smart, but I am God smart, and THAT matters more than anything.

As you read through this diary, it will take you on a journey of how my legacy began. It shares with you what I went through emotionally, spiritually, and physically, to accomplish what God desired for me. Oft times we move and make decisions based on how we feel, what we think, where we are in life, and what we think we should have based on the goals established by society. What I found out on this journey is that God does not move according to our will; He moves according to His will, plan, and purpose for us. In other words, our blessings come from being obedient to His plan. When I started, I thought I was on task with the Lord, and I soon found out that I was *slightly* off. I bless God that I know His voice, I hear His voice, and that I am obedient to His voice – even when it goes against the very desires within me. I know that His way is better than mine, and I will reap greater rewards when I sow my life in obedience.

I pray that this diary helps you to fulfill your purpose according to God's perfect plan, and that you are blessed beyond all you could ever imagine or think.

THE PLEA

Dear Diary,

First, I want to thank God for this day. For waking me up this morning, and positioning me to see a new day. It is a beautiful sunny morning, and I can hear the birds singing outside my window. I am up and in full swing of my day.

I am super excited to go into my newly remodeled ultra girly shabby chic bathroom - the blue lace walls and Halifax cream bead board brings me peace in the morning. The mirror finish on the outside of my claw foot tub makes my pedicure look flawless. Lord, I love my new bathroom.

After washing my face and brushing my teeth I took a good look at my face - God has graced me well, I will be thirty-five tomorrow, and no wrinkles.. I have to give the Lord a shout of praise for keeping me looking fine. But I cannot help but ask Him, where is my husband He promised me I would have? I thought I would have him by now. My 35th birthday party is tonight, and I have NO date, no one to share this milestone with. Tomorrow, it's official... I will be a 35-year-old VIRGIN!!!

All my friends have husbands, wives, and families. He gave Chastity three husbands and four kids - I just want one and one. Please hear my prayer, oh Lord.

The highlight of my day, after I made my usual tea and toast and retreated to my comfy couch to watch the morning news, I noticed a new mail carrier approaching my door. I quickly jumped up and opened the door before he could knock. He was fine. I mean – whew! I felt something *tingle* fine! Lord, help me! He had honey colored legs with hairs all laying in the same direction. His uniform shorts fit just right, and his chest made his uniform shirt look like a well-pressed military uniform. Luscious! I quickly pulled my robe closed to hide my torn t-shirt and my ex's Raven football pajama shorts. He looked at me, flashed those beautiful pearly white teeth, and said, "Ma'am, I need you to sign for this letter." I was blinded by love at first sight - I didn't hear a word he was saying. His heavenly glow had me mesmerized; and, I almost could see our wedding day, until I noticed as I handed him back the letter and pen, he was wearing a diamond wedding band. DANG, another one taken. I slammed the door in his face. I felt like all the air had been sucked out of me, death destroyed my dream, and he could read my thoughts. Then I hear him say, "nice hair!" I turned to my left, looked in the mirror, and noticed my hair was standing up like unpicked wheat. I quickly brushed it down with my hand, returned to my comfy couch, and opened the letter. Well, it seems I have to return home once again for the reading of Papa's will. My heart began to pound so hard and so loud, it sounded like the bass in my jam, MTume's, "Juicy Fruit." I reminisced over the melody... "I like it, I like it, yeah."

I dread having to go to New Jersey once again; I just left all the drama, and got my head back right since the last visit. (Bursting into song) "Oh Lord, I need you to help me." I'm not really looking forward to this visit, but Papa was all I had, and now he's gone too. I know that Sandra and Darnell are my cousins, but I feel like I have no family left. We are a very small family, and I do wish we were closer, or at least civil to one another.

I truly love and appreciate my Grandparents for all they have done for me. I had a great childhood, even better teen years, and great support from them until their last breaths. My anxiety flares when I think about reuniting with my cousins, Sandra and Darnell. I always felt that they were spoiled and disrespectful. When my Grandmother died ten years ago, they carried on at the funeral like they were burying their parents all over again. I know death can be traumatic - but really, it was a bit much. I remember Sandra bawling and clawing my Grandmother in the casket. Then she jumped back

15

like someone was supposed to catch her, and she slipped and fell right under the casket. Good Lord, her dress blew up and the undertaker quickly ran over and took off his jacket to cover our unrequested showing of all the goodies. I still get a little giggle when I think about it. Darnell was yelling in this high pitched, yet deep, heart-wrenching tone that sounded as if someone was torturing him. "Noooooo, stop, come back, I cannot make it..." All I could think about was the way they treated my Grandmother. Guilt is why they put on such a show. Mama was a beautiful woman; her perfectly finger waved gray hair fell just past her shoulders. She had high yellow skin with olive undertones, silver around her front side tooth, and when she smiled, she lit up a room like sunshine. She was medium build and still had a nice shape, I believe my good genes come from her. She aged gracefully with integrity, despite how Sandra and Darnell treated her and Papa. Papa was average height, he had the biggest smile, yet you could only see the rim of his teeth. He had deep dimples and was the perfect shade of honey, and his silky grey hair was like Billy D. Williams. He worked hard to provide for us. Well, now he too has gone on to be with the Lord. Sweet rest, Mama and Papa.

I expect this to be my final trip to "Misery City." First - I am off to get my first birthday present from my girl, Lee Lee. A complete day of relaxation at Trinity Total Body Salon & Spa. Yeeesss, as I inhale and exhale deep breaths to the thoughts of a full body massage, foot massage, get my nails and hair done, and then it's off to shop at my favorite store - Bloomingdales!!!

I'll be back later to share about my day and night. Lord, I pray I meet Mr. Right somewhere along my day. Remember me Lord.

LET ME FILL YOU IN: Chastity was my college roommate; she and I have remained good friends. She is a native of Detroit, and stayed in Florida after we graduated college. She met and married her college sweetheart, who became a NBA player, and whose career ended just as fast as their marriage. They had one child together. She then married her second husband who was killed in a motorcycle accident while she was pregnant with her second child. She is now married to a brilliant attorney, who loves and adores the ground she walks on. They have two children together.

Dear Diary,

Lord, I thank you for another glorious sunny morning. Thank you for the breath of life, and thank you for last night! Happy Birthday to me!!! I hear the spirit of the Lord saying that He is going to heal the land. I am not certain what that means, now, but I plan to petition God to find out.

Last night was my birthday celebration! My natural tresses were swept up into the perfect pompadour, my nails blinged out with 3D diamond nail art, and I had on the most amazing dress - Lee Lee hooked me up! That's my girl. I wore a Diane von Furstenberg midnight blue sleeveless, side slit dress with a round neck, sheer yoke, and hem, with embellishment all over it. For accessories, I wore pink and white chandelier earrings that rested just above my shoulders with Badgley Mischka "Giana" Metallic Peep Toe d'Orsay Pumps, with a pink satin clutch. I looked good. I felt good. Oh, and my party… Let's just say it was fantabulous, darling!!!!

I've always known that I am one of the top backing vocalist since I came on the scene. My 5-octave range has afforded me the opportunity to back up some of the best of the best in the music industry; but last night, love proved to me that it is an action word. I am still amazed by who all showed up: Pastor Dale Ciceron was the MC, and everyone came - Uncle G, Alexis Spight, Kirk Franklin, David & Tamela Mann, Anita Wilson, Tasha Cobbs, Lowell Pye, Karen Clark Sheard, KiKi Sheard, Maurette Brown Clark, AJ Brown, Bubby Fann, Lucinda Moore, Paul "PDA" Allen, Pastor Jason Nelson, Ron Grant, Apostle Veryl Howard, Todd Dulaney, Deitrick Haddon, Queeni, and my church family of course; they showed up, and showed out! I was in tears as Earl Bynum and the Mount Unity Choir sang their hearts out. Pastor William McDowell set the atmosphere, Will Brown and Another Level took us to another level, then Alexis, Tasha, and Lowell took us to the next dimension. "Amazing" is an understatement of just how God moved through that place. Lord knows, last night is what I needed to get my mind off of the fact that I am thirty-five, alone, a virgin, and I have to go back home next week to deal with Papa's estate.

Now that I think about it, Lee Lee is the woman that made it all happen. Mrs. Latarshia Adams is more than a high profile entertainment attorney; she is definitely my closest friend. I love her like a sister. It is still amazing to watch how her petite frame, preppy vernacular, and proper posture meshes with that gangster swag and slang talking husband of hers. I wonder what her twins are going to be like when they start talking? Latreecia Monae, and Prince I'jay Sun Adams, Jr. - hahaha I laugh every time - what was his mother thinking? Well she did something right. He did attend Cornell University, he graduated, and has a solid income as a teacher. Basketball scholarships can produce more than just NBA players. He is a good person, a good father, and he is good to my sister-friend.

At least she has someone. My last boyfriend and I broke up right before Papa died. Now, I feel disconnected from men. All he wanted was to get me into bed all the time. Why can't men respect my decision? Why couldn't he just respect my commitment? I only want to share my body with my husband. I have kept my vow and virginity since I attended Purity Classes at Papa's church. I want my life to be different, so that means, I have to do something different. When I have my children, I want them to be different, spirit-led different. I guess that's why I'm alone, and holding on to a childhood vow.

Lord, I keep reminding you of your promise; when are you going to fulfill it? I heard you say you are healing the land, but Lord please do not let my next birthday be alone. I am tired of coming home to this big four-bedroom house, alone. I have renovated all three bathrooms, built me an amazing 400 square foot closet, and the contractor comes on Monday to start on my new kitchen. Lord, fill this house with a family - I want a husband and a baby, or three. Please Lord, that is all I want for my birthday.

Dear Diary,

I bless your name Lord for this new day, thank you for the rain - now I don't have to water the grass. Saving a few coins before I spend a small fortune is always a blessing.

Church was off the charts today! The choir is growing spiritually, and the praise is going higher and higher. It is so amazing! I like the new keyboard player; he understands the vision God has placed in me for the music ministry. It's like he can see which way my soul goes - and he follows every note, riff, and run. I can feel his soul tapping into the melody of mine, sweet beautiful chords manifest, and we go higher spiritually. We're a match made in music heaven.

I gave him a ride home today after service. Poor thing, he loaned his car to his friend who totaled it. Such a nice guy, doing a nice thing, and look how something bad happens. Just like the devil - always trying to stop and block progression in the Kingdom. He asked me when was I going to record my own cd? I told him that God hasn't revealed that for me to do just yet, and I will let him know when He does because he understands me, musically. It's like he is inside the melody, riding with me. "Ooo la la la" I can hear Teena Marie singing… "it's the way that you feel when you know that it's real."

Lord, this is my daily reminder to you…. please make this year my year? Thank you.

Dear Diary,

Lord, you did it today. I got asked out on a date! Well, not actually a date - just to a music session with Quwan. He asked me to come and see if I want to write to a new song he is working on. Lord, you know that man moves things in me I did not know could move. Lord, if this is him, thank you.

Dear Diary,

Session was amazing!!!! I felt God moving in me, like He wrote the words, and projected them out of me. I've never written a song before. Nevertheless, the music we made this afternoon was unbelievable. Quwan is so talented; he plays keys, drums, bass, and rhythm guitar – man, if he can play the sax, I may propose to him. He asked me to attend the Stellar Awards with him. I told him, he can come with me as I will be on stage. I also told him, it would be a great opportunity for him to network with some major artists. We decided that we would meet there since I have to leave a week early for final rehearsals.

It should be fun as he and I are really becoming good friends. It's actually nice having a male friend. Maybe he can tell me what I am doing wrong, and help me find a husband? Alternatively, maybe, he will be my husband - Quwan Fleurnoy and Mikayla Howard-Fleurnoy - that don't sound too bad.

Lord, remember me!

Dear Diary,

It's a rainy day today; I pray the weather is better in Jersey. I'm only going because I must. Chastity is late, as usual, to take me to the airport. I'm not mad either - she has all those adorable babies - Lexon, Zion, London, and Leroyce Jr. I wonder what happened to the new mail carrier - I haven't seen him in a while. Lord as I travel back home today please be a hedge of protection around me. Take me, keep me, and bring me back home safely. In the name of Jesus, I pray. And Lord, please, please, please do not let me see "you know who." Our last run-in was very awkward. Amen.

Remember me Lord, this is my year.

TAKING CARE OF BUSINESS

Dear Diary,

Lord, first let me acknowledge you for always having a sister's back. Smooth take off, flight, and landing - thank you, thank you, thank you!

Well I'm here, settled into the hotel. I could not fathom the thought or energy to stay at Papa's. One reason is that all the memories always seem to keep rushing back, flooding my heart, and my mind with an intensity so strong I can barely breathe. Second, Sandra and Darnell are there - they never seem to have a job, money, or initiative to get anything. Anyway, I am not sure what Papa is leaving them. They only lived with us for four years, and they never came back after they left for college. They didn't even come to help take care of Papa when he got sick. Tomorrow, we'll find out. I think I'll hire an Estate Auctioneer and Realtor to sell the house. I have no plans to move back or visit. There is no one here I want to see, either!

Dear Diary,

Lord, forgive me. I have sinned. Not only have I sinned, but I sinned with "you know who." I broke my promise to you, Lord. I said I would never see or entertain him again. I meant it Lord, you know I did. I only opened the door because I had ordered room service, and there he was standing, a 6'4" tall glass of dark chocolate, eyes twinkling, skin glistening, and that infectious smile. The way he licks those soup coolers, and bites the corner of his bottom lip; always makes me weak at the knees. His six-pack makes his shirt ripple in all the right places... then, BAM! From behind his back he swings a dozen luscious red roses in my face and says, "Happy Belated Birthday!" I am so caught off guard all I can say is "oh, thank you." He says "You're welcome. Aren't you going to invite me in?" as he's walking past me. His boss swag is one of the reasons I fell in love with him. That same swag dragged my heart across a bed of razor blades, I quickly remind myself. When I turn around, he is already making himself comfy on the couch. I ask, "How did you know I was here?" He said Darnell told him. Broken glass of orange juice, geesh can he keep a secret, ever???? We talked, and I must say it was okay. This was the first time I did not feel like placing my - well let's just say, I did not have the urge to cause him bodily injury. He got straight to the point and apologized for our last run-in. All I wanted to know is how he ended up with my closest childhood friend, my sister-friend, Myesha? Now he is sitting here saying that it was an accident. He claims that when Myesha and Rodney broke up; she got drunk, he thought he was being a brother, and making sure she got home, and the next thing he knew, "*it*" happened and she was pregnant. I could not hold it. "So, you found out the morning after?" He said, "Well No, but it happened so fast that it felt like it did." He went on to apologize and say that he never meant to hurt me, that he had no choice; and I should understand that knowing how his parents are, he had to marry her. My mouth moved on its own again "did it mean you had to be happy too? I'm just asking because you two did not look like the "we had to get married" couple?" He said, "you know you crazy, and what kind of question is that? You know that we have always been friends." He went on to say that he came to apologize and to make peace with me because Myesha needs a real friend right now; she has stage 2 breast cancer. That broke my heart more than anything. She and I were closer than friends, we were sisters! I grabbed my purse and said, "let's go." We went to the hospital, we cried, we laughed, we prayed, we made peace. I told her I will come see her tomorrow afternoon to check on her after her surgery in the morning. Lord, I pray you cover my sister and heal her body in the name of Jesus. Now I am heading over for the reading of the will. Lord, be a fence around me. Clothe my mind and heart with joy and love. In Jesus name, Amen

I'll be back later with an update.

LET ME FILL YOU IN: Mr. "You Know Who" is the oldest of six children born to a Pastor of a very prominent church in Plainfield, NJ. His parents were very strict, and well respected in the community. His father was very active in social justice, and education issues. His mother was always very missional; founding several food pantries and shelters for homeless veterans and families. All of their children followed their life blueprint: graduate college, marriage, and then children. Although his parents are both deceased, he is still very mindful and respectful of his upbringing.

Dear Diary,

Lord, I cannot believe all that happened today. My mind is simply blown away! Let me start from the beginning. The law offices were very contemporary in design. Glass walls and exotic wood tables, colorful canvases of abstract art and sculptures everywhere. There was so much to take in; very classy and engaging. The attorney was dressed very business chic. She had on a basic pencil skirt, a jacket tailored to her every curve, and the fit was impeccable - like a master tailor crafted it to her body. I cannot forget that her shoe game was right up my alley - Jimmy Choo

Anouk pump. Love him for the design, and her for rocking them! She was thorough and professional. Papa left the house to me, which I have known since I was twelve. What I did not know was that Papa was worth MILLIONS!!!!! $30 million to be exact! I also didn't know he had millions tucked away for Sandra and Darnell from the death of their parents, and for me from my mother. One meeting and we were all millionaires. But God! One thing I love that he did is put everything in one pot, and divided it evenly amongst us so no one would be mad. I got the house because it was purchased with money from my mother's death. The other thing I found out is my father's name. Yes, and I am even more blown away because today I found out that Myesha and I are half sisters... we have the same father. I wonder if she knows???? Well I plan to visit her parents anyway to find out who knows what? Wow! Mr. LeBlanc is my father. He was always nice to me, and I'm figuring that he must have known something. Myesha's surgery went well, and she is resting peacefully. I plan to be here for the next week, at least, to settle business.

Thank you Lord for this day. Thank you for the life of my Papa. Thank you for equipping him with integrity. Thank you Lord, for keeping Myesha and me today. In Jesus name I pray.

Dear Diary,

Good Morning Sunshine! I fell asleep on the sofa gazing over the city lights. The wall of windows and curtains are wide open and my room is beaming with sunshine this morning. I love the crisp white linens on the bed and the warm gray micro suede tufted headboard. The silver and bronze accents add just enough bling and zen balance to the room. It's very relaxing. I think the older I get the more I evolve into the more classic contemporary design and furnishings. I have a full day of errands, conference calls, and most important, my meeting with Mr. & Mrs. LeBlanc. I called them yesterday when I left the lawyer's office, and they said I can come by for lunch.

Lord, thank you for waking me up this morning revealing your sunshine. I look forward to a good day with you. In Jesus name, Amen

Dear Diary,

Day 2 of Mind-Blowing Facts: Apples really don't fall far from trees. I have heard my grandmother say that down through the years but today I saw it; bright and vivid like the yellow sun that I awoke to this morning. Revelation is as bright and beautiful as sunshine. Yes, James LeBlanc is my Father; his wife Mabel is my aunt. Papa really was a rolling stone. Mrs. Mabel LeBlanc and my mother were best friends, and sisters. I asked Mrs. Mabel if my mother knew they were sisters and she said that she did. They were not allowed to share that publically because my grandmother was not aware of Papa's "secret love child." Apparently, when my mother died giving birth to me, my father turned to my aunt for comfort and they ended up falling in love and getting married. Now today I find out that Myesha is not only my best friend, my sister, my real sister, but also my cousin - who is now married to "you know who" —— my first love, my high school sweetheart. Ugh! She is just like her mama…

Today was a real eye opener for me. I always thought that Mr. LeBlanc was just looking out for me because my grandparents were older, and his daughter and I were best friends. Now I know, he is my Dad. It feels weird because I have known him all my life - so I have always known my father, just not the fact that he was my father. I am not certain about my feelings just yet, there is still an emptiness in me, and this is a lot to take in.

Well Lord, it is time to get some sweet rest, today my brain and heart has labored more than I wanted them to. Lord, help me to digest all this information and progress forward. Be with me Lord, I have to stay longer than I planned. Lord, please remember me - this is my year!

Dear Diary,

I will bless the Lord at all times, His praise will forever be in my mouth. Lord, I thank you for the best night's sleep I have had in a very long time. This morning I feel refreshed and renewed. Today I will meet with the Realtor, the Stagers, "you know who," & Myesha. Lord, be with me as I go about my day, direct the words that come out of my mouth, and take lead on every decision, in Jesus name I pray. Amen

Life Lesson: You don't really know people until you ask questions, and see them in their own land.

Dear Diary,

Well, the Realtor had nothing but "get ready to write the check" news - tons of work is needed at the house. The stagers quote was ridiculous - I can beat that price renting from Aaron's; but the topper of the day was I let "you know who" take me to lunch. I am not sure how to feel about him. The conversation was good; we talked about old times - good years, many laughs. Then, he apologized, again, for breaking up with me when I left for Florida State. He said that he was young, immature, and afraid that I would fall in love with someone else, give up my virginity, and break his heart - so he broke mine first - TWICE!!!

Lord, thank you for being with me and speaking for me - I know it was you that spoke those forgiving and kind words, the Holy Spirit is doing a great work in me. I must say, I felt completely at peace about the situation. Oft times I make decisions based on my fears, not realizing that God is control of all things, and what He wills will be. Lord, thank you for the right-now healing you gave Myesha - the doctor said all cancer was removed, a few Chemo sessions and she will be as good as new.

I didn't talk to her about the new revelations I have experienced yet, I will be here for, at least, another two weeks so we'll have time to talk about everything.

WHEN LOVE CALLS

Dear Diary,

Today was a very interesting day. First, I got a call from Lee Lee. She said she misses me, and for me to hurry home. My assistant called frantic because the one of my upcoming weddings is over budget and the bride wants only to speak with me. Weddings are my passion, but the brides - ugh - I can do without all the drama. They are emotionally in over drive all the time – EVERYTHING is an emergency. Then, Quwan called me and said that he misses me too - that was sooooo sweet - he made my morning tea and toast taste better. Something about that man makes me smile on the inside. Lord, I am still waiting for the answer. Is this my husband?

The highlight of my day was the contractor - Jacob aka Mr. Dreamy! Jacob Alon Matthews, owner of JAM Construction. Fine is an understatement for him. He is gorgeous! He's a skyscraper next to me standing at 6'5"; a former professional football player. I googled him. He was an All

American in high school, an alumni of FSU (like me), a Heisman Trophy winner, and #1 NFL first round draft pick by the Dallas Cowboys. He set tons of records over his pro career so he is a future NFL Hall of Famer, and has two Super Bowl rings. Whew - he is more than a mouthful of water - he is a bathtub FULL!

Well anyway, Mr. Dreamy was an absolute gentleman; he was patient, walked me though all the work that needs to be done, and gave me a written quote on the spot. Efficient, a man after my own heart. He was talking to me, and honestly I do not have a clue what he said - I was in la la land for real. I could see him as my husband. Jacob Matthews and Mikayla Howard-Matthews - I like the sound of that! Lord, I pray he did not over charge me - I said yes to everything he said, including dinner tonight. YES!!! I have a date with Mr. Dreamy.

I called my girl Lee Lee and she said for me not to dress too sexy, and not to tell him I am a virgin on the first date. Then she went on and on about not getting lost in his words and doing too much upfront, and ga ga ga and ma ma ma - I lost track after a while. I know she means well but I am grown, I am capable of making my own decisions, and obviously, I am doing very well. My business is a huge success, and no one has been able to break my virginity to date. Anyway, I know she only wants the best for me, and wants me to remain level headed. Lord with your help, I will.

Lord, thank you - this is my year!!!

Dear Diary,

Lord, thank you for waking me up this morning. There's something about the rain in New Jersey that always make me feel nostalgic. I remember me and Myesha putting on our rain boots and jackets and playing in puddles of water. We would pretend we were on Broadway and dance and sing down the sidewalk – "singing in the rain, we're singing in the rain…" hahaha good times, good times. Myesha and I have so many great memories together and nothing can take that away. I love her to life for life. "You know who" called me and said Myesha took a turn for the worst last night. Needless to say, I rushed to the hospital to be by her side. Jacob graciously drove me, and stayed with me until 5 am. As I sat there in her room, holding her hand, watching the rain drops hit and run down the window, I felt a humming in my spirit of "Swing Low, Sweet Chariot, coming forth to carry me home." The tears were running down my face, and as each drop hits my lap, it is as if my tears are keeping time to the song. I could literally feel her life slipping away. All of a sudden she began to shake uncontrollably. I screamed for help and "you know who" runs out the door - a hundred people rush through the door. We were pushed into the hallway while they were working on her. We tried to see what they were doing, but there were so many people in the room we simply couldn't. "You know who" drops to his knees and cries out to God, "please don't take her now, please not now Lord, I need another chance - to get it right, to make things right - I promise I will do it, Lord please." His pain saturated the hallway, I fell to my knees beside him and comforted him, and Jacob comforted me. The doctor finally came out of the room and said, "She is alive, but in very grave condition. We will move her to CCU, but I must advise you, if she makes it through the night - it will be a miracle."

Lord, you are the giver of life to everyone and everything. I will your will, have your way Lord, right now in the name of Jesus, Amen.

Dear Diary,

"You know who" just called and said that she made it. She is still in CCU, on life support, and still critical, but she's still here. Lord, I thank you for every moment of my life and every moment of the lives of all the people I love. Lord, her life is in your hands, your will will be done in Jesus name, Amen.

Jacob and I will meet today so I can give him the deposit. I will be flying home today; I have to get back to work. I now have two brides that do not understand I am entitled to a personal life.

Lord, I thank you in advance - this is my year.

Dear Diary,

Lord, I thank you for this day. It's good to be home. Both weddings were a success and most importantly, within budget. Praise God. Brides can be a handful in planning and even worse when they are over budget.

Here comes "Mr. Already Married." Every day he brings my mail to the door now. Ray Charles can see he's married; wearing a polished diamond wedding band. He's always waving it in my face as he hands me my mail...that's why I always slam the door in his face. I think he enjoys it; he just chuckles and says he'll see me tomorrow. Ugh. Why me Lord? Please do not give the enemy permission to agitate me. I have enough on my plate.

It has been brought to my attention, while I am running back and forth to New Jersey, that Quwan has proved himself the typical man. He has four baby mamas, including "Quiet Karen," and now Beverly is pregnant by him. Needless to say, I was floored. Now I know why Karen left the choir when he was brought on staff.

Lord, we all need deliverance in some area of our lives. Help us, deliver us, and heal us in the name of Jesus I pray. P.S. Lord, I thank you in advance, that this is my year! P.S.S. Lord, I need a miracle today. I am watching Leroyce, Jr. for Chastity, and you know I do not know anything about watching kids. Be with me Lord, I need you.

Dear Diary,

Well I made it, barely, but I made it. L.J. is 18 months old. The Nanny had death in her family and will not return until tomorrow. Chastity had an important meeting and begged me to come and watch him. Well, I didn't get the memo that babies' poop smells like raw sewage, and will run out of the diaper. He and I went out for a little trip to pick up some last minute things needed for an event. He is really well behaved so I figured it was no big deal. Well, to my surprise… He STINKS! I mean bad, and I did not bring the diaper bag in the store with me. I asked the sales person to show me to the baby section so I could get some stuff to change him. I had no idea the baby selection would be so overwhelming, all the boxes and numbers. I grab the box for 10-14 lbs., and rush to the bathroom. I take all the stinky stuff off and discard it in the trash. I put him in the sink and washed his butt off, and then I try to put the pamper on him. It's not fitting. A nice woman comes in with her son, who is around the same age and size as L.J., and she says, "here try this one?" This pamper fits perfectly. I explain to her that I am babysitting, and forgot to bring diapers with me.

I told her that I grabbed the box that holds 10-14 lbs. of waste, and she began to laugh hysterically, then she finally says that 10-14 lbs. are the weight of the child, not amount of waste. I laughed with her and told I have no kids, and obviously no clue. I guess this is why the Lord placed me in this position to see - I am not ready! Chastity thought it was hysterical too! Lesson learned, and I plan to spend more time around kids so I can learn and grow from the experience.

Lord, help me. I want to be ready. Remember, this is my year!

Dear Diary,

Lord, I thank you for safe travels, I pray your loving arms sustain and keep me. Lord, I see now that you have not forgotten me.

Well, I am back in New Jersey to meet with Mr. Dreamy regarding the progress on the house repairs. After the walk through, he asked me out to dinner again. This seems to be our normal routine when I come to town. He really is a gentle giant, and always a perfect gentleman. He opens doors, pulls out chairs, and even when I've tried, he always pays for dinner. I enjoy talking with him, nightly, before bedtime and his wake up messages every morning. I would say, in my Roberta Flack/Lauren Hill voice "He's killing me softly with his song, killing me softly, with his song." I love this man and he doesn't even know it. We have been seeing each other for a few months, and I want him to do things to me that I never wanted from any man before. It is amazing to me that the opportunity never presents itself for me to fall - not that I want to fall into sin - but I want to; I wrestle with my flesh when I see him - he must be the one. He is so easy to love, and he honors my vow.

Lord, help me… this is my year!

Dear Diary,

Last night there was something different about Mr. Dreamy, it was as if he wanted to tell me something; he seemed a bit on edge. He called when he got in his car and said that he wants to tell me something, but he is not sure how because he is not sure he should feel this way about me since we are not "technically" in a relationship. I encouraged him to tell me. Finally, he says, "I love you. "I placed the phone over my heart and said, "Thank You Jesus" - I could hear him saying, "Hello? Hello?" I picked up the phone and said, "I'm here, are you sure?" He said with no hesitation at all, "Yes, I'm very certain. I cannot stop thinking about you. I want to spend the rest of my life with you." I said to him, "is this a proposal for marriage?" He said, "Yes, I believe so." Just then, I heard a knock on my hotel room door and it was him. I opened the door and he grabbed, and kissed me and whirled me around saying, "yes, yes I want to marry you. I have never felt like this with any woman, or man, and yes I want to marry you." Wait... Did I hear him correctly... did he just say he never felt this way with any other woman or MAN???? I guess the expression on my face told him that he needed to explain to me what he meant. He said, "That did not come out right, I mean that I have never loved anyone like I love you - not even my mother or father or brothers or sisters, nobody." Oh ok, that calmed my fears of him being gay. Then he kissed me and I think I saw Jesus nod his head yes, this is the one, and then I said, "YES, I will marry you."

Thank you Lord. I knew this was my year!

Dear Diary,

Lord, I cannot believe I am finally engaged. It has only been a few months since my birthday, and I am on track to be married by my next birthday, and maybe even have a baby on the way soon. Jacob respects my vow, and will wait until we are married to have sex. I told you, he is the perfect gentleman.

Thank you Lord!

Dear Diary,

Jacob flew to Florida and took me to meet with a jeweler to design a custom engagement ring for me. WOW! Who does that? For me? I selected the color, shape, size, and the setting. I chose something extremely unique, something that I never saw before. I selected a cushion setting surrounded by heart diamonds alternating in direction, and all four corners have a princess diamond that will sit a little higher to hold center stone in place. The band is a half circle of round diamonds with a round center diamond on each side finished with an extra thick platinum band so it has a snug fit to sit in place. I cannot wait until it is finished, all 10 carats!

Thank you Lord. Embracing my year!

Dear Diary,

The Lord's will, has been done! The wedding plans are coming along great; David Tuterra is a God send. He understands my "lofty" plans and has designed my wedding as if he was inside of my head. As much as I love Florida, my home, I have agreed to move back to New Jersey, since Jacob's business is based there, and I can work from anywhere. I will spend the next week in Jersey working on the plans for our June wedding. That was strategic to get married in June because I plan to be pregnant by my birthday next September. Yes, the Lord knows what He is doing and I thank Him every day. Our colors will be black and various shades of pink with silver accents, and bling. The centerpieces will be a variety of tall and short glass vases with volumes of Calla Lily, Lily of the Valley, Gardenia, Gerbera, Hyacinth, Iris, Hydrangea, and Roses. Yes, I went over budget with the flowers. Thank you Papa! We will have custom linens and overlays with accents of diamonds. Diamonds are a girl's best friend, as I raise my hand and admire my custom 10 carats of diamonds that will soon be delivered. He is a great man and I am falling deeper in love with him. He sends me messages every morning to start my day, he touches base with me during lunch, and we talk for hours from dinner to bedtime. Well, I better get packed; I will be leaving in two days to be with my fiancé!

Lord, I thank you for healing the land; you do it again and again.

Dear Diary,

Lord, I thank you for this day, I thank you for safe travels, the plane encountered some turbulence, but by your grace, I arrived safely. It amazes me that as we are approaching Thanksgiving, all I see is Christmas decorations. Advertisers are making their push for Christmas sales earlier and earlier every year.

I am excited to meet more of Jacob's family, Myesha and "you know who" will be coming from my side of the family. I thought about inviting Sandra and Darnell, and then I quickly rethought, and opted not to do it. My girl, Lee Lee and her family will be coming as well. She said she has to give the stamp of approval. He's the one and I know it! Not only does it feel right, but everything is flowing right. Thank you Lord!

Dear Diary,

I never thought I would be back in Papa's house. Jacob did an excellent job restoring this old Victorian to its former glory, and the stagers have tastefully decorated with a blend of old and new furnishings. While I was waiting for the realtor to come and take some pictures, someone came by looking for Jacob. He said he saw "J's" car so he thought he was here, and wanted to drop off some keys to him. I gladly offered to take the keys, he said, "Are you the Realtor?" I said, "No, I am Jacob's fiancé, may I ask who you are?" He said, "I'm a client. He's doing some work at my house, and I was on my way to drop the keys off to him. Here, you can give them to him? Tell him they are from Danny." He handed me the keys and left. Thank God, the realtor finally arrived, and we finalized the contract. The house is officially on the market. I have mixed emotions about selling the house. I have a lot of great memories here. Myesha and I used to slide down the bannister when Mama called us down from my room to eat. I remember one time we were sliding down the banister and I fell off half way down and rolled down the stairs. Thank God, I was alright. Speaking of Myesha, I am late for our lunch date, and meeting with David for dresses. TTYL

Dear Diary,

I had a very productive day yesterday; Myesha and I had a great time shopping for bridal party dresses with David. That man is simply amazing, and I am so honored to have him as my planner. Thanks Papa - because of you I can really afford him! Myesha is currently in remission, and in excellent spirits. My niece is growing by the second and is so smart, four going on forty! Later I met up with Jacob for dinner, he seemed a little down. I asked what was going on and he stated that business has been a little slow lately. I gave him the keys from Danny, and offered to spot him some money. We are getting married so what's mine is his, and what's his is mine, right!? He said he was okay in the financial department. He was unusually quiet during dinner and decided to call it an early night. I guess he has a lot on his mind; I know I do. A lot has to be done this week while I am here, and Thanksgiving is in two days. Well, I better get some sleep. GN

Dear Diary,

I was up early yesterday morning to pick up Lee Lee and her family from the airport. We're staying in the same hotel, and her parents are watching their children so this is a getaway for them. Lee Lee is excited about it. I was excited to see my custom masterpiece. It's perfect, just like Mr. Dreamy. Thank you Lee Lee for picking it up, guarding it with your life, and safely delivering it to me.

Lee Lee and I went over to Myesha's to do our part of the cooking for Thanksgiving. We were having a great time making desserts, admiring my newly be-diamond hand... until they started in on me with 21 Questions about Jacob. How are things going? What's his family like? Are there any baby mamas? They just went on and on and on. Especially Lee Lee, she cross-examined me as if I was on the witness stand. Tomorrow will be the first time I meet his family which is why I wanted them there with me. No kids that I am aware of; well, now that I think about it - I never asked, and he never said. So I sent him a text kind of jokingly asking about kids. He quickly replied, "Yes, two boys 13 & 15, they live in Dallas with my ex." My eyes got wide as saucers, and my heart began to race. I felt faint. Apparently, it was all over my face and Myesha asked, "What's wrong?" "He has kids, two boys..." I blurted out and sat down immediately wondering, who am I marrying? Do I really know him? Yes, I do. He is gentle, kind, and loving. He is the perfect gentleman and he respects me. What more do I want from a man?

Jacob came to my hotel, and we stayed up half the night talking. He officially placed my engagement ring on my finger, and I feel like I know him better. We talked about his childhood, how he was raised, his college adventures, and his NFL career. We talked about where we want to live, and how we will manage our bills and income. He even agreed to a Pre-nuptial agreement. That was a first for us, and I enjoyed it immensely. Oh, and contrary to popular belief we were not bored at 5am - we ordered room service and took a nap. I felt safe in his arms as we snuggled on the couch together.

He left to get dressed for the evening. My girls and I arrive promptly at 6 o'clock for dinner. I rang the bell, and his father answered saying, "Which one of you beautiful ladies is my future daughter-in-law?" I raised my hand toward him to show off my ring with a big smile on my face and said, "Me!" He smiled and said, "Come here, gal!" He gave me a huge country hug like I was family he had not seen in a long time. We went in, and I quickly made myself at home. I began to help setting up and serving as the woman of the house would. His mother was quiet and very observant. Like his father, his siblings were very welcoming and engaging. It was priceless watching all the men eating and watching football. I thought to myself, "This is my future husband and our future Thanksgivings."

Jacob's house is a very contemporary 3000 square foot open loft, with exposed brick and duct work, black high gloss kitchen cabinets with white Carrera Marble counter tops, top of the line stainless steel appliances, including a 6 burner Jenn-Air stove with griddle and multiple convection ovens. I cannot wait to cook in that kitchen. His oversized leather sectional accommodates seating comfortably for, at least, ten people. His love for Black Art is shown through his extensive collection. His taste is totally opposite of my shabby chic style. We're going to need a designer to merge our styles. It was a beautiful evening, and our families got along very well. He has a large family, and he's the third eldest of eight children. Today it was clear to me why he said he would pay for 70% of the wedding. Oh yeah, his client Danny came by with his partner. They were nice and fit right in as if they knew us all for a long time. He was friendlier than our first meeting.

After everyone left, his mother, sister, and I were in the kitchen cleaning up and his mother said to me, "Do you think you two know each other intimately enough to get married so soon?" I assured her, "yes, we have a very open and honest relationship built on mutual respect and love." She hummed a gritty, " Mmm Hmm, we'll see." His sister said, "Mom, that is not for us to decide. They're both adults. Jacob knows what he's doing. Besides, I think he got it right this time." Jacob brought me back to my hotel, and on the ride I asked him why his mother asked me that? He said, "It's cool babe. She is over protective of her children, and is always looking to see if someone wants me for me, or for what I have." I said, "Did you tell her I have my own?" He said, "Yes, no worries." Then he grabbed my hand and kissed it. He is so sweet. He did not linger too long tonight. He was heading out to meet up with his brothers to play pool and catch up.

Dear Diary,

Thank you Lord for safe travels. It feels so good to be home. Not that I don't love being in Jersey, but my bed is super comfortable, and I miss my couch and morning meditations on it. There is truly no place like home. The mail carrier shows up today and tells me that he missed me; "Really??" I said, and shut the door in his face as always. He yells, "I hope I see you tomorrow." Ugh! Why me Lord?

No sooner do I slam the door that I receive a crazy phone call from some woman stating that she has four children by Jacob. I say to her, "This sounds like a conversation you need to have with Jacob. Why are you calling me?" She replied, "Jacob never wants to claim my kids because I was a prostitute, my kids are a reminder of his darker days." Again, I reminded her that she needs to talk to him and not me. I hung up and called Jacob, he said that he has a stalker and to block the number. He said that he filed a complaint against her, and a judge ordered her to jail time. She recently got out and is at it again.

Lord, I pray he is telling me the truth. This is not a good start to merging our lives together.

Dear Diary,

That woman called me again - this time from a different number. She told me she is with Jacob and asked me if I wanted to listen to them have sex? Lord, you know it took everything in me to not go slap off on this stalker chick – (but she laid the phone down and I listened - I do not know why - but I did.) I never had intercourse with Jacob so I am not sure how he sounds in bed... she only referred to him as J – and that could be anyone. I hung up and called Jacob. He didn't answer. He called me back about 20 minutes later and said that he was in the shower. I told him about the phone call, he told me to block her number, and that he would handle it. Now, I know I should not doubt him, but I am starting to question him. Lord, I have been waiting so long for a husband; I have kept my vow, and I kept myself only for my husband. Please do not take me anywhere you do not want me to go. In Jesus name I pray, Amen.

Dear Diary,

It is 3:00 a.m. She's calling me again from a different number. This time she said nothing - she is having sex in the background and saying, "Give it to me, harder J, harder J... Yes, yes..." then silence... I could hear moving around, then the music was almost faint and a door closed. She then said, "You may have the ring, but I have the man." She hung up.

I called Jacob, he answered and he sounded like he was asleep, this calmed my nerves. He said he spoke with his attorney and legal action will begin again against this woman. He promised me that he was handling it, but it takes time. I asked about the four kids, and he said that he has paternity test results to prove he is not the father of any of her children, and she has been stalking him since his NFL career started. He said that he was young, he fell for the groupie sex one time, she was the girl, and she has been harassing him ever since for child support, visitation, and whatever else she could conjure up.

I want to believe him but with every call, I am losing faith. Lord help me.

Dear Diary,

Something weird happened this morning, the mail carrier introduced himself to me. Why in the world would I care that his name is Dwayne? I am engaged to a wonderful man who may be cheating on me with his stalker. But, I am in a good place now.

Jacob told me he only has two children by his ex who lives in Texas. Maybe I should give her a call and calm my fears? Maybe I should hire a private investigator so I know who I'm marrying. On the other hand, maybe I should call his Mother and find out if this is the reason why she was so shady towards me? Maybe she knows something about this stalker chick. My mind is racing, and my thoughts are all over the place. I don't know what to do, or where to turn. Since I started receiving the phone calls from the stalker chick, I have noticed that Jacob is not calling as much. I cannot help but wonder if she is telling me the truth? Is Jacob cheating on me with someone he calls a stalker? He has never lied to me, as far as I know... and has always assured me I can check his phone, use his phone, and answer his phone at any time. Why am I worried? He asked me to marry him! He chose to give me his last name... Lord forgive me for the thoughts of explicit language.

Dear Diary,

I was awakened by Dwayne. He's really getting on my nerves. I think his daily life depends on messing with me.

This woman is relentless. She called every hour last night; always from a different number. She must be using one of those internet apps. I didn't answer her calls and I didn't call Jacob either. If there is anything going on, it will reveal itself. I don't believe the Lord will bring me this far and leave me. Right, Lord???

Dear Diary,

It has been a while since I had a chance to chronicle my journey. There has been so much going on I can barely keep up. Since I met David Tuterra, the two of us have become great friends, and he has been sending me some work so I can transition my Event Planning business to New Jersey. God bless that man! Jacob and I are still moving forward with our wedding, and we found a beautiful 5000+ square feet, six bedrooms, and seven-bathroom house in Mendham Township. Jacob plans to rent out his loft in Jersey City and Papa's house sold for above asking price.

Life Lesson: You shall receive a harvest if you never give up.

I thank God I never gave up on my beliefs, my commitments to myself, and I am thankful for a man who respects me for them.

Dear Diary,

I have been turning my phone off at night now, and sleeping a heck of a lot better. This stalker is not giving up so easy. Jacob is coming to Florida for Christmas. I have to pick him up from the airport at 11:00 pm; he's flying in from Texas. I am excited to see him. Whenever I am going to see him I get butterflies in my stomach. I feel like a little girl on her birthday waiting for her gifts.

I better get going; I have a few stops to make before I pick him up.

Dear Diary,

Jacob called me so I could meet his boys via Face Time – they're handsome and tall - just like their Daddy. He said he has to reschedule his flight so he can attend an event with the boys. He did not stay on the phone long, but now he will arrive two days AFTER Christmas. This totally sucks! I have cleaned the house, ran around, and delivered all my gifts, prepared a special meal for him, and now he cancels. I understand, yet upset at the same time. He has never done that before. What is going on so special in Texas? I bet he is hooking up with his ex, or maybe the stalker chick is there and he wants to spend a few more days with her before he comes to see his future ball and chain. WTF...

Dear Diary,

I have been up all night with the phone on waiting for his call; it never came. I have called him several times and his phone is going directly to voicemail. Where is he? Did something happen to him? Is he with another woman? I cannot do this - this has to stop!

Dear Diary,

So, Jacob is a liar. He arrived at my home this morning with his boys. SURPRISE! They drove here from Texas all night. He said he broke his phone, and a new one was going to be delivered to my house today. SURPRISE is an understatement. When that doorbell rang, I thought it was Dwayne - but it was Jacob - bringing me my mail, and his boys, so I could meet them in person. He made arrangements for us all to stay in a massive suite at Disney. This was all a part of his plan for their Christmas. He gave me a beautiful Secret Wonder necklace by Harry Winston. He has excellent taste in jewelry, hotels, and food. I am falling deeper and deeper in love.

Oh yes, his phone arrived just like he said. I can relax now.

Dear Diary,

His boys are amazing. We had a great time. They were very well mannered young men, and we all got along great. That is such a relief. I was worried about becoming a Step Mother. It's not so bad. It took a moment for his younger son to open up, but once he did, we had a blast. The boys will fly back to Texas by themselves, and we will fly back to New Jersey together. We have final plans to review for our new home, and more wedding plans to finalize. I am looking forward to bringing in the New Year in New York. All the years I have lived in New Jersey I've never gone to Times Square for New Year's Eve. This will be a first and I am so happy to spend it with my love.

Dear Diary,

I'm not sure if it was fatigue or something's wrong, but Jacob was very quiet during our plane ride. He seemed a little pre-occupied with getting his phone set up. He has never been super protective about his phone with me, but I did notice that he activated the finger print lock/unlock feature. I tried to unlock his phone and noticed that he changed the passcode that he had on his previous one. Is he hiding something from me? Why did he change the code? I haven't heard from the stalker chick in a while. Is there any truth to them being in a relationship? I don't like this feeling; something I've never felt before. I'm not sure how to proceed with him. I don't want to appear that I am insecure or that I do not trust him, but I am not sure how to feel, or what to do? I want to be married, to him, and I don't want to do anything to blow it. I will just keep my mouth shut and see what unfolds. Mama always said what is done in the dark will come to light. The truth will eventually make an appearance and all will work out. Right????

Dear Diary,

Jacob gave me the new code, I checked his phone, and there was nothing there. Not that I exactly know how to work an Android phone – I'm a Mac girl, but I feel better.

New Year's Eve in New York was magical. I feel like we got closer, and I like this feeling.

We met with the architect and the renovation plans are in motion for our new house. We interviewed several potential designers to help merge our styles. Thank God, he is very contemporary and I am very Shabby Chic. This is going to be very interesting.

Life Lesson: Do not get lost in him, you still exist.

Dear Diary,

Apparently, stalker chick was in jail for violating the no contact order. She was released today, and I guess the calls will soon start again. I really don't want the drama as we head into the "Love" month. I'm already nervous. We're going away for Valentine's Day. I don't want to get weak and give it up before we say "I Do!" I'm not sure where we are going? I was instructed to pack a weekend bag of toiletries only. This makes me uneasy. Where are we going? Why can't I bring clothes? Will we be wearing clothes?

Be right back - the phone is ringing

That was Jacob, his son was injured, and he has to fly to Texas today. I pray all is well with his son. I need him to answer some questions for me about our upcoming trip.

Dear Diary,

I have not heard from Jacob, and I pray all is well with his son. Lord, cover him with your blood and bring healing in the name of Jesus I pray. Amen

Dear Diary,

Jacob called early this morning. His son had to have emergency surgery. Right now he is stable and expected to make a full recovery. Jacob plans to stay until he is home, and then he will come to Florida to spend some time with me here before we head out on our mystery trip. I guess I'm not big on surprises; I am definitely struggling with this one.

I haven't seen Dwayne lately. I wonder what is going on with him? The new mail woman is nice, a little lazy - she doesn't bring my mail to my door.

Dear Diary,

Stalker chick had the audacity to call me and say she is in Texas at Jacob's mother's house. She said that they are good friends and get together several times a year. She hung up. I tried calling the number back - no answer. I called Jacob, and he stated that his parents are with him at the hospital visiting with his son. I can't help but wonder; are they really there? I should have asked to speak to his father; I don't think his mother would humor me with a hello. Would Jacob lie about his parents being there? Do his parents live close to their grandchildren? Will I ever go to Texas to his parents' house? Will I ever see where his children live? Hmmmmm, I'm wondering.

Dear Diary,

Stalker chick sent me a picture of her bikini bottom and legs on a deck overlooking a pool. WTF? This has to stop. I am going to hire a private investigator when we get back from this trip. I have had enough. As far as I know, he has never lied to me - but something is going on.

Lord, please forgive me for my explicit thoughts. This has carried on long enough; I need answers.

Dear Diary,

Valentine's Day was a co-ed weekend with my closest friends and their spouses for a Couple's Wedding Shower. It was beautiful. Jacob is so sweet. He arranged everything. I had my own hair and makeup squad as well as a rack of Edmond Newton custom designs. We had a couple's massage that were so relaxing. I had to do a lot of praying. I saw my future husband's body, his naked body, and he is cut in all the right places. My, my, mine!!!!

Dear Diary,

We are three days away from moving day, and three months from being Mr. & Mrs. Jacob Matthews, Sr. OMG! We are about to move in together. What if I fall, and get pregnant? If I have a son, he cannot be a junior. I feel myself hyperventilating. I grab the wall and Jacob catches me - asking if I'm alright. I began to rattle off all my anxious thoughts and concerns about moving, the new house, meeting with the designer, the wedding, and having children. Jacob assures me that everything will be alright. This is the right thing to do and fear is not an option now - the movers are scheduled, the house is purchased, and the wedding date is set. I know he's right, but I am feeling so weird lately. Stress. Occasionally, I still have the creepy conversation in the back of my mind that I had with his mother on Thanksgiving. I have tried calling her a few times since then so we could get to know each other, and she refuses to get on the phone - but Dad is super cool. All the phone calls from stalker chick leads me to thoughts of her showing up at our door. What will I do if she does show up, or worse, if he does not come home at night? This is also a tough month to move, Mama died in March - maybe that is why I am on edge. Lord, you know!

THE ASSESSMENT

Dear Diary,

I do not understand Jacob, but I love him. I'm here in New Jersey full time now. We are going to be married in two months, and he is becoming more and more distant. He moved in the house with me, but stays on the other side of it. He is working extremely long hours, and sometimes all night He says that he wants to get ahead so we can go on a four-week honeymoon. He is so sweet, always looking for ways to spoil me, and make up for lost time.

Dear Diary,

Myesha came over today to see the house. She and I had a weird conversation. She said to me, "You are a smart woman, always keep your eyes open in marriage; signs are everywhere." I asked her what she meant by that? She said she just wants me to be alert and notice any changes in his behavior - emotionally and physically. I told her things are well, he is working a lot so we can go on a long honeymoon - but other than that, things are great with us. I cannot help but wonder if she was trying to tell me something, without telling me.

I have to fly back to Florida in the morning to check on my house. I plan to rent it out. I'm sure I'll get great renters since I live so close to Disney.

Dear Diary,

I feel very weird today…. I received a message from Lee Lee; she said, "Walk into the light Carol Ann, what's up with you? I have not heard from you since you got your ring. Call me, we need to talk." (What does she mean - walk into the light Carol Ann??) That girl is crazy! Who is Carol Ann?

Then, I saw two messages on Twitter that spoke to the inner me…

@speaktostacy un-forgiveness is an emotional indication that you want to remain connected to the source of your offense (this speaks to "you know who" for me)

@realtalkkim God cannot bless who you pretend to be (am I pretending to be me?)

Bishop George Bloomer was on TV saying that "when a man finds a wife he finds a good thing" is a scripture often misinterpreted. A man can only find a wife if he has seen one. If he has never seen a wife, how will he know he has found one? How will a woman know she is a good wife if she has never seen one (interesting)?

How do I know I am a good wife? I know what Mama used to do - but is that what I will do? Is that what I should do? Was Mama a good wife? Have I ever seen a good wife?

Once again, I feel faint, the room is spinning, and I feel life is spinning out of control. I heard the Lord say, "be still and know that I am God." LORD!!!!!

Please tell me I am not wrong Lord?????

I have been waiting a long time to find love, to be engaged, to get married, to have children. Lord NOOOOOOOO, please do not take this all away from me. What will I tell my friends? How will Jacob respond? All the money that has been spent on the house, the renovation, the wedding, and flying back and forth to NJ. Lord NOOOOOOO!

Dear Diary,

Needless to say I did not sleep well the past two nights, I have not spoken to Jacob, and I have been in deep prayer and fasting. I have wanted these moments so desperately for so long, and now that it is within my grasp, it all appears to be slipping away.

The question is: Should I allow my desperation for my dream life to lead me out of the will of God for my life?

I have to pray! Lord, I desperately need direction.

LIFE LESSON: I do not need a man; I want a man. But, God wants me with the man He ordained for me. Be still. Slow down. Seek God for direction. As I read the last few entries, I noticed God has been missing. I am out of order, and out of alignment with God. I need to take a step back and re-align with the will of God for my life.

DELIVERANCE

Dear Diary,

It has been quite some time since my last entry. Clearly, I was in a moment of desperation and despair. Decisions needed to be made about my future. Do I pursue the life I have always dreamed about, or the life God desires for me? I have been in deep prayer, fasting, and embracing my process to who God called, and desires me to be. Today, I am happy to share the answers have come, and some very tough decisions have been made.

I am no longer getting married.

I am no longer with Mr. Dreamy.

I am no longer bound to my dream life.

I am embracing a life in the will of God, the life He desires for me. I was moving so fast that I got ahead of Him and what He wants for me. His plan is better than my plan. This was not an easy decision for me; I wrestled with God. Everything I ever dreamed about was on the table spread before me like Thanksgiving dinner. Yet, all the things that I dreamed about could not fill the emptiness.

I began to lose myself in my dreams, in Jacob, and I no longer could see God or myself. The Bible says in James 1:22-25(NIV)

Do not merely listen to the word, and so deceive yourselves. Do what it says. Anyone who listens to the word but does not do what it says is like a man who looks at his face in a mirror and, after looking at himself, goes away and immediately forgets what he looks like. But the man who looks intently into the perfect law that gives freedom, and continues to do this, not forgetting what he has heard, but doing it--he will be blessed in what he does.

I desire to be a doer of the word; I want His will for my life. Lord, I apologize for allowing my desperate mind to step ahead of your will, plan, and purpose for me. Lord, please forgive me as I forgive anyone who has sinned against me. Help us all to walk in your righteousness.

I had to take some time in prayer and fasting. I took time to dissect our relationship - individually and collectively.

Pros and Cons of our Relationship.

PROS: loving, gentle, perfect gentleman, caring, family-oriented, a great dad, close family even though they live miles apart, hard working, thoughtful, and respectful

CONS: he has a stalker, or is possibly cheating on me, his mother is shady toward me, I am not sure I know him as well as I think I do, and I do not completely trust him.

Who Brings What to the Table?

Jacob has: his own business, owns a loft home, co-owns a home with me, has two children (one of which is already a Jr.), has a stalker (or may be cheating on me), has stable finances (unsure how much, we never disclosed finances to each other); the elephant that I did not want to see in the room - he practices Islam.

Mikayla has: her own business, backing vocalist to major artists in Gospel industry, owns a single family home, co-owns a home with Jacob, no children, multi-millionaire through inheritance, I practice Christianity, a church girl, God fearing, a virgin, desperate for God's leading and directing.

TRUST - NO

LUST - YES

What do I want more than anything else? To be in the will of God

What does he want more than anything else? I have no clue

What are our Long-term Goals?

Mikayla: I want to franchise my business so I can travel as a professional singer; have the flexibility to stay at home and raise my children, record a cd, go to church as a family, raise my children in the church, take mission trips, live a Holy life, make it into heaven.

Jacob: he wants to own multiple rental properties, flip four properties a year, travel with his sons, attend their college games, and help them obtain their NFL dreams, no more children, have a happy wife, and a happy life.

What Is Our Five Year Plan?

Mikayla: Married, three children, settled and happy, following God's will, plan, and purpose for our lives.

Jacob: Traveling with his sons, successful business, and a happy wife.

Communication: I heard him, but I thought I could change him. I thought I was strong enough in my faith to win him over to Christ. He has never thought about going to church with me, much less verbalized it. We have had conversations about many things; however, now I see that I wanted to get to know him, and he rarely asked about me. How is there a "we" if I know about him and he knows nothing about me? He never asked!

What We Have in Common:

going out to dinner

stable finances

entrepreneurs

traveling

Differences:

Mikayla: I want to travel with a singing career, I want children, and I want us to go to church together - serving Jesus

Jacob: to travel with his kids, no more children, expand his real estate portfolio

Eye Openers:

I am consumed by him. Where am I in this relationship? Where is the relationship?

We are unequally yoked. We serve two different Gods.

I have more to lose, losing me is more valuable than gaining him.

I do not know him as well as I think I do

We are traveling toward two different destinations

We do not have enough common denominators to balance each other out.

After I finished my assessment, I laid before the Lord in silence, seeking Him for clarity, for answers, for peace. Surrendering my being to Him, acknowledging Him at the wheel.

I heard the Lord say to me, "be patient, he is not the one." These words rang louder and louder with each day as we came closer to me becoming

Mrs. Jacob Alon Matthews, Sr. I felt physically ill at times.

As desperate as I was for my dreams to come true I realized that I am more desperate to be in the will of God. I have to see him for who he is, and me for who I am. There is no thread strong enough to keep us together. Together meaning - walking together toward the same goals at the same time.

The Bibles says in 2 Corinthians 6:14- 17(NIV)

Do not be yoked together with unbelievers. For what do righteousness and wickedness have in common? Or what fellowship can light have with darkness? What harmony is there between Christ and Belial? Or what does a believer have in common with an unbeliever? What agreement is there between the temple of God and idols? For we are the temple of the living God. As God has said: "I will live with them and walk among them, and I will be their God, and they will be my people."

Therefore, "Come out from them and be separate, says the Lord. Touch no unclean thing, and I will receive you."

I asked God what must we agree on - His answer, "Me."

WOW! We have to agree on God. My mind was blown. If our foundation is poured with different materials (Gods), at different times; we are separate. Even though we stand side by side; we are neighbors.

I now understand Chastity, she always said that we women have to see men for who they show us they are, and listen to what they say. Their actions back their words; we are the ones that normally give in to have them.

She said to me, "Anyone can be there; but, who is going to be there when life is turned upside down? Who is going to be there drinking sweet tea with you on the front porch after the kids are all grown and on their own? Who is going to stand with you when it all falls apart?" My answer was GOD! He said in His word that He is with me always even until the end of time. He has proven time and time again and has stood the test of time.

This is not my time. This is not the man. I can accept defeat in this moment naturally because the next moment is my true victory. That is the moment I realized the error of my ways and realigned myself with the will of God. Now I can press on with my head high, unmoved by the opinions of others, and that is spiritual victory over my natural soul.

God is the lover of my soul and I yield to His will from this day forward. Lord I thank you for revealing yourself to me, for revealing Your will to me, and for forgiving me for getting in the way of the me You have called me to be.

Life Lesson 1: I may not be where I want to be in the world, but I am exactly where I need to be with God.

Life Lesson 2: Losing me is more valuable than gaining him.

Life Lesson 3: I must be in love with the present him not the idea of him!

TRUE DESTINY

Dear Diary,

Thank you Lord for this new day. Thank you for waking me up this morning. Thank you for supplying my every need. Thank you Lord for everything. Is someone really ringing my doorbell at 7:00 this morning? Lord, I pray it is an emergency because it is too early for foolishness!

Dear Diary,

It took a minute for me to get back to you because it was "you know who" at my door? My initial thought - What is he doing here? I had to pause for a second, make sure my hair was not standing up on my head, adjust my robe just right to show a bit of skin, then I opened the door. "Good Morning" he says with that silly grin on his face. I asked him, "What are you doing here? How do you know where I live? Wait... don't answer that." we said together - "Darnell." We laughed, and then I said, "But, please answer my first question - what are you doing here?" He asks, "Can I come in?" "NO!" I immediately replied. I was not properly dressed to entertain company so early in the morning. I asked, "Is everything okay with Myesha?" He immediately replies, "NO!" and he bursts into tears. He quickly walks past me, and began to tell me how the doctors have discharged her to hospice. He brought her to Florida so she could die in peace, and to be near her one and only friend, and sister; that was her only request. I am crying and whisking through the house, yelling back to him let me get dressed so I can go to her. When I came back into the living room, he was sitting there with his face in his palms, sobbing and apologizing. He shared with me that he has never stopped loving me, that no matter how great a wife and mother Myesha was, she always knew that he was in love with me. They were going to counseling when Myesha was diagnosed with cancer. He said that he married her because she was pregnant, and figured that love would come... over time. Love had developed, but not the kind of love that married people share. When she took ill he felt that God was punishing him. He said that if he had another opportunity at a life with her, he would do everything he could to love her, as a husband should. I held his hand, and put my arm around him to console him, and he leaned in and kissed me. I pulled away, went into my bedroom, and locked the door. I am hurt and relieved at the same time. I always wondered if he ever loved me, and if he still did? I also wondered if he loved my best friend, my sister like he loved me, or more? A rush of fury came over me. I began to pace back and forth asking how he has the audacity to come here, crying, and saying all this stuff now? Myesha is dying. "WE ARE NOT A PING PONG GAME!" I shouted from the top of my lungs. I prayed and got myself together, and returned to the living room fully dressed and said, "I'm ready to go." He wanted to drive me but clearly, he was in no condition to drive anyone, anywhere.

We arrived at the hospice facility. It was very nice, and it felt like a resort. Myesha was awake and although she was weak, she managed to smile and say, "Hi beautiful." Much to my delight, I embraced her with a huge hug, and told her how much I loved her and that nothing would ever change that. Then she apologized to me, the tears began to flow from both of us. She shared with me that she never meant for anything to happen between her and Miles. That when she found out she was pregnant, Miles being the man of God he is, did the right thing, and they got married. She said that she always knew that he never loved her like he loved me. She even said that one time he called out my name while they were having sex. She always knew he was still in love with me, and no matter what she did she could never compare to me. She began to cough, and she squeezed my hand tighter as she covered her mouth with the other hand. Once she got herself together, she said to me that she wanted to come to me because she wanted to ask me a very important favor. She said, "I want you to help Miles raise our daughter." I quickly said, "Yes, yes, I will…whatever you want." She said to me, "One more thing, please marry Miles, he loves you." I was in such shock; I could not respond. She squeezed my hand again, and I felt her spirit leave her body.

Dear Diary,

I am still in shock over the request of Myesha. I am not sure what to do; I am laying before the Lord for the answer. In the meantime, today we will spread the ashes of my sister, my best childhood friend, as she requested in the ocean.

Lord give us strength to stand in this hour!

Dear Diary,

Today was a tough day, Miles, M'Kai, and I. We set out to sea on a private yacht to scatter Myesha's ashes on the sea. We said a prayer, and cried together. Miles and I were almost at the point of kissing, and I pulled away. It felt right, but I couldn't do it, it is too soon. We had dinner on the yacht, and spent the remainder of the evening in silence.

Lord, I need you to direct me... singing in my Queeni voice, "I will your will have your way."

Dear Diary,

It has been several weeks since my last entry; Miles and M'Kai have rented a house here in Florida, and plan to stay close so I can help. Miles and I have had many long talks, and he confessed that he is still in love with me, and that he never stopped loving me. He said that although he married Myesha, he knew that she knew how he felt about me and that was always a point of contention in their marriage. He apologized again, and I apologized to him as well. Holding a grudge is never the right thing to do. The word teaches us to forgive others, or our heavenly Father will not forgive us. I told him we can take it slow and rebuild our friendship first.

Dear Diary,

Today Miles and I went on our first formal date! We took M'Kai to school, and then headed over to the park. We walked and talked for hours, grabbed lunch, and before we knew it, it was time to pick her up.

Today was a great day! Lord thank you for leading me into my destiny.

Dear Diary,

Well, it has been a few months since my last entry. As you probably can imagine, Miles and I have fallen in love with each other again. We are preparing to celebrate M'Kai's 5th birthday, and we plan to be married Thanksgiving Day. We are eternally thankful for all God has done for us, and in us. We look forward to what God is going to do through us.

Won't He Do It? Yes, He Will, if you let him!

Dear Diary,

"True love never dies" - Stacy Lattisaw was so right. I have always loved Miles, he has always loved me, and together we have always loved the Lord.

This journey was not easy as I reflect through the previous entries, but God! I made it – God's way. No, I did not get married and have a baby on the way by my 36th birthday, but I am definitely, where God wants me to be. I am happily married to my first love, Miles Jackson Carpenter. We are proudly parenting our daughter, M'kai, and expecting twins on my 37th birthday.

P.S. Now I understand what the Lord meant by healing my land.

2 Chronicles 7:14(NIV) if *my people, who are called by my name, will humble themselves and pray and seek my face and turn from their wicked ways, then I will hear from heaven, and I will forgive their sin and will heal their land.*

When we are called by God, and submit to Him, we must pray and seek His will, plan, and purpose. We must turn from our own agendas, desires, wants, and in our obedience the Lord will forgive our missteps, and heal us from the inside out.

Listen to what God says to you. Do not think you can change a man - only God can do that.

Stay in the submission position to the Lord so you can receive all that He has for you.

The Bible says: Jeremiah 29:11(NIV) For *I know the plans I have for you," declares the Lord, "plans to prosper you and not to harm you, plans to give you hope and a future.*

YOU BETTER BELIEVE IT!!!!

THANK YOU

I pray that you enjoyed the journey of my desperate attempt to gain it all; the husband, the big house, and the children. There were moments when I did not want to hear God, but His persistent call eventually had to be answered. I am eternally grateful that I came to my senses and answered before I was in a situation that I would regret for the rest of my life.

Life is not easy, the enemy is always tempting us, but the good news is found in 1 Corinthians 10:12-14

12 So, if you think you are standing firm, be careful that you don't fall! 13 No temptation has overtaken you except what is common to mankind. And God is faithful; he will not let you be tempted beyond what you can bear. But when you are tempted, he will also provide a way out so that you can endure it.

I pray that you received just what God wanted you to get, so you can embrace life as He desires it for you. Trust me, life is better obedient.

ABOUT THE AUTHOR

Pastor Queeni is an energetic and anointed Domestic & International Gospel Recording Artist. She penned and released her first CD – "Queeni presents…Sunday Morning" (2006) with music by Darin "Pianoman" Whittington (Brittney Spears, Changing Faces, Quincy Jones, Mary J. Blidge). She later penned her second CD – "Grateful" (2010) with her group NJ Praise, with music produced by Darin "Pianoman" Whittington, Franklin "Bubby" Fann (hit songwriter/producer of "Judah Praize", Marvin Sapp), and introduced new music producer, Daniel Grant.

This multifaceted performer has performed all over the continental United States and internationally in Korea, and 15 cities in Italy. Pastor Queeni has shared the stage, toured, and worked with top entertainers in various genres of music including: The Temptations, Donnie McClurkin, Deitrick Haddon, Joe Pace, Bubby Fann, Dorothy Norwood, The World Famous Harlem Gospel Choir, Chic Corea, Roy Ayers and countless others. Pastor Queeni made her acting debut in 2009 as the leading lady in the stage play "First Lady" written and directed by Carmen Davis of Head of My Life Productions. In 2013 she played the leading lady in the stage play "Once Was Blind" written & directed by Emmy Award Winning Producer, Glenn Barbour, Sr.

Pastor Queeni's start in music was a divine assignment to prepare her for ministry. Over the years she was running from the call from God and experienced many trials and tribulations. Pastor Queeni struggled with two failed marriages, one broken engagement, and two miscarriages. She came to a pivotal point in her life where she had to ask the tough questions, she submitted herself to God, and He provided the answers. Pastor Queeni accepted her truth, realigned herself with the will of God, and married the man God desired for her. After moving to Orlando, FL, in 2010 she answered the call into ministry with a resounding YES!

Pastor Queeni has been blessed with many gifts and talents and wears many hats including: Event Planner, Event Producer, Vocal Coach, Graphic Designer, Mentor to new Pastors and Entrepreneurs, Founder of Queeni Sings Ministries, Co-Owner/President of Inspiration Music Group, a Mary Kay Cosmetics Senior Consultant, Host of "The Story" Radio Show & TV Show, the Founder and Pastor of River Of Life Christian Worship Center in Howell, NJ, and now Author of her first book, "Diary of A Desperate Mind." She is a devoted wife, a loving mother to a blended family of eight children, and she is the "Madea" to nine grandchildren.

Pastor Queeni's quote for life is Reach, Embrace, and Enjoy - Reach for what God is calling you to do, Embrace every opportunity to serve, and Enjoy every blessing for your obedience!

CONTACT THE AUTHOR

M. Queeni Green
Queeni Sings Ministries
P.O. Box 2
Browns Mills, NJ 08015

www.queenisings.com
Info@queenisings.com